ERIC CARLE
Pancakes, Pancakes!

by Eric Carle

READY-TO-READ

SIMON SPOTLIGHT
New York   London   Toronto   Sydney   New Delhi
This book was previously published with slightly different text.

SIMON SPOTLIGHT

An imprint of Simon & Schuster Children's Publishing Division

1230 Avenue of the Americas, New York, New York 10020

Copyright © 1990 Eric Carle Corporation

Eric Carle's name and logo type are registered trademarks of Eric Carle.

First Simon Spotlight Ready-to-Read edition 2013

SIMON SPOTLIGHT, READY-TO-READ, and colophon are registered trademarks of Simon & Schuster, Inc.

For information about special discounts for bulk purchases, please contact Simon & Schuster Special Sales at 1-866-506-1949 or business@simonandschuster.com.

The Simon & Schuster Speakers Bureau can bring authors to your live event. For more information or to book an event contact the Simon & Schuster Speakers Bureau at 1-866-248-3049 or visit our website at www.simonspeakers.com.

Manufactured in the United States of America 0313 LAK

First Edition 10 9 8 7 6 5 4 3 2 1

Library of Congress Cataloging-in-Publication Data

Carle, Eric.

Pancakes, Pancakes! / by Eric Carle. — 1st ed.

p. cm. — (Ready-to-read)

This book was previously published with slightly different text.

Summary: By cutting and grinding the wheat for flour, Jack starts from scratch to help make his breakfast pancake.

[1. Pancakes, waffles, etc.—Fiction. 2. Cooking—Fiction.] I. Title.

PZ7.C21476Pan 2013

[E]—dc23

2012017343

ISBN 978-1-4424-7274-7 (pbk)

ISBN 978-1-4424-7275-4 (hc)

This book was previously published with slightly different text.

Kee-ke-ri-kee!

A rooster crowed.

Jack woke up and thought,

"I want a pancake."

Jack said to his mother,

"Can I have a pancake?"

"You can help me make it,"
said his mother.
"First we need some flour."

"Cut some wheat, please.

Then take it to the mill

to grind into flour."

So Jack cut the wheat.

Then he went to the miller.

Jack asked him

to grind the wheat.

First they had

to beat the grain

from the wheat.

"Now we will grind the grain
to make the flour,"
said the miller.

Jack helped the miller

to make the flour.

Then he took

the flour home.

"Can we make a pancake?"
asked Jack.

"Now we need an egg,"
said his mother.

So Jack got an egg

from the hen house.

"Can we make a pancake?"

asked Jack.

"Now we need some milk,"

said his mother.

So Jack milked the cow.

"Can we make a pancake?"
asked Jack.

"Now we need some butter,"
said his mother.

So Jack churned
some butter.

"Can we make a pancake?"

asked Jack.

"Now we need to make a fire,"

said his mother.

So Jack got some firewood.

"Can we make a pancake?"

asked Jack.

"Now we need some jam,"

said his mother.

So Jack got some

strawberry jam.

"Can we make a pancake?"

asked Jack.

"Yes!" said his mother.

So Jack and his mother

mixed everything in a bowl.

They put some butter

in a hot pan.

"Jack, now put some

batter in the pan,"

said Jack's mother.

Jack's mother

cooked the pancake.

Then she flipped it.

The pancake flew up high.

It landed in the pan.

Jack's mother put the
pancake on a plate
and gave it to Jack.
Jack said,
"Mama, I know
what to do now!"

CANOPUS IN ARGOS: ARCHIVES

Re: COLONISED PLANET 5

SHIKASTA

CANOPUS IN ARGOS: ARCHIVES

Re: COLONISED PLANET 5

SHIKASTA

Personal, Psychological, Historical Documents
Relating to Visit by **JOHOR** (George Sherban)

EMISSARY (Grade 9)
87th of the Period of the Last Days

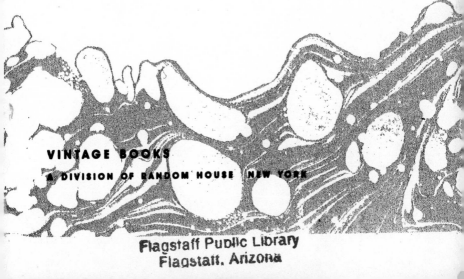

VINTAGE BOOKS
A DIVISION OF RANDOM HOUSE NEW YORK

Copyright © 1979 by Doris Lessing

All rights reserved under International and Pan-American Copyright
Conventions. Published in the United States by Random House,
Inc., New York. Originally published by Alfred A. Knopf, Inc.
New York, in October 1979.

Library of Congress Cataloging in Publication Data

Lessing, Doris May, 1919-

Shikasta : re, colonised planet 5.

I. Title

PR6023.E833S54 1981   823'.914   81-40194

ISBN 0-394-74977-4   AACR2

Manufactured in the United States of America

98

BVG 01

For my father, who used to sit,
hour after hour, night after night,
outside our house in Africa, watching
the stars. "Well," he would say,
"if we blow ourselves up, there's plenty
more where we came from!"

Shikasta is the first of a series of novels
with the overall title *Canopus in Argos: Archives.*
The second will be *The Marriages Between Zones Three,
Four, and Five.* The third will be *The Sirian Experiments.*

SOME REMARKS

Shikasta was started in the belief that it would be a single self-contained book, and that when it was finished I would be done with the subject. But as I wrote I was invaded with ideas for other books, other stories, and the exhilaration that comes from being set free into a larger scope, with more capacious possibilities and themes. It was clear I had made—or found—a new world for myself, a realm where the petty fates of planets, let alone individuals, are only aspects of cosmic evolution expressed in the rivalries and interactions of great galactic Empires: Canopus, Sirius, and their enemy, the Empire Puttiora, with its criminal planet Shammat. I feel as if I have been set free both to be as experimental as I like, and as traditional: the next volume in this series, *The Marriages Between Zones Three, Four, and Five*, has turned out to be a fable, or myth. Also, oddly enough, to be more realistic.

It is by now commonplace to say that novelists everywhere are breaking the bonds of the realistic novel because what we all see around us becomes daily wilder, more fantastic, incredible. Once, and not so long ago, novelists might have been accused of exaggerating, or dealing overmuch in coincidence or the improbable: now novelists themselves can be heard complaining that fact can be counted on to match our wildest inventions.

As an example, in *The Memoirs of a Survivor* I "invented" an animal that was half-cat and half-dog, and then read that scientists were experimenting on this hybrid.

Yes, I do believe that it is possible, and not only for novelists, to "plug in" to an overmind, or Ur-mind, or unconscious, or what you will, and that this accounts for a great many improbabilities and "coincidences."

The old "realistic" novel is being changed, too, because of influences from that genre loosely described as space fiction. Some people regret this. I was in the States, giving a talk, and the professor who was acting as chairwoman, and whose only fault was that perhaps she had fed too long on the pieties of academia, interrupted me with: "If I had you in my class you'd never get away with that!" (Of course it is not everyone who finds this funny.) I had been saying that space fiction, with science fiction, makes up the most original branch of literature now; it is inventive and witty; it has already enlivened all kinds of writing;

and that literary academics and pundits are much to blame for patronising or ignoring it—while of course by their nature they can be expected to do no other. This view shows signs of becoming the stuff of orthodoxy.

I do think there is something very wrong with an attitude that puts a "serious" novel on one shelf and, let's say, *First and Last Men* on another.

What a phenomenon it has been—science fiction, space fiction— exploding out of nowhere, unexpectedly of course, as always happens when the human mind is being forced to expand: this time starwards, galaxy-wise, and who knows where next. These dazzlers have mapped our world, or worlds, for us, have told us what is going on and in ways no one else has done, have described our nasty present long ago, when it was still the future and the official scientific spokesmen were saying that all manner of things now happening were impossible—who have played the indispensible and (at least at the start) thankless role of the despised illegitimate son who can afford to tell truths the respectable siblings either do not dare, or, more likely, do not notice because of their respectability. They have also explored the sacred literatures of the world in the same bold way they take scientific and social pos- sibilities to their logical conclusions so that we may examine them. How very much we do all owe them!

Shikasta has as its starting point, like many others of the genre, the Old Testament. It is our habit to dismiss the Old Testament altogether because Jehovah, or Jahve, does not think or behave like a social worker. H. G. Wells said that when man cries out his little "gimme, gimme, gimme" to God, it is as if a leveret were to snuggle up to a lion on a dark night. Or something to that effect.

The sacred literatures of all races and nations have many things in common. Almost as if they can be regarded as the products of a single mind. It is possible we make a mistake when we dismiss them as quaint fossils from a dead past.

Leaving aside the Popol Vuh, or the religious traditions of the Dogon, or the story of Gilgamesh, or any others of the now plentifully and easily available records (I sometimes wonder if the young realise how extraordinary a time this is, and one that may not last, when any book one may think of is there to be bought on a near shelf) and sticking to our local tradition and heritage, it is an exercise not without interest to read the Old Testament—which of course includes the Torah of the Jews—and the Apocrypha, together with any other works of the kind you may come on which have at various times and places been cursed or banished or pronounced non-books; and after that the New Testament, and then the Koran. There are even those who have come to believe that there has never been more than one Book in the Middle East.

7 November 1978 —Doris Lessing